# LABOR

Jill Magi

# LABOR

NIGHTBOAT BOOKS
BROOKLYN & CALLICOON
NEW YORK

ISBN: 978-1-937658-14-4

Cover, title and interior page art and photography: Jill Magi
Courtesy of the artist

Design and typesetting by Margaret Tedesco
Text set in Bell Gothic, Courier, and Garamond

Cataloging-in-publication data is available
from the Library of Congress

Distributed by University Press of New England
One Court Street
Lebanon, NH 03766
www.upne.com

Nightboat Books
Brooklyn & Callicoon, New York
www.nightboat.org

*And would shout it out differently*
*if it could be sounded plain;*
*But a mouth is always muzzled*
*by the food it eats to live.*

*Martin Carter,* "A Mouth is Always Muzzled"


*I don't want to suggest that the position of the outsider is always or*
*only negative, or necessarily critical, or bound up in envy, a yearning*
*for an inside position. The outside is capable of great positivity*
*and innovation.*

*Elizabeth Grosz,* Architecture from the Outside


*I think I have a vague desire to be alone, just as I realize I've never*
*been alone anymore since I left childhood behind, and the family of*
*the hunter. I'm going to write.*

*Marguerite Duras,* The Lover

Work,
as cultural expression,

day as unit of,
distinction between, and hobby,

distinction between, and leisure,
distinction between, and slavery,

domestic,
domestic, as resistance,

domestic, devaluation of,
as gendered practice,

home-based,
and identity,

imaginative,
leisure and,

non-wage,
pace of,

patterns of,
and pleasure,

as pleasure,
as social self.

Workers,
commodification of,

factory,
female,

false consciousness of,
restructuring bodies of,

seasonal,
textile,

and artists,
cooperative and,

ritual,
unionized.

See also Wage labor,
Labor activists,

Labor,
Department of,

Division of Negro Labor,
Women's Bureau,

Labor or trade unions
and Communism,

black women,
as leaders of.

Work ethic,
Work force,

polarization of,
marginalization of,

working wives,
work patterns,

*Work and its Discontents.*
Workplace resistance,

absenteeism,
deference and,

feigning of illness,
footdragging,

negligence,
networks of solidarity,

organized resistance
and quitting,

sabotage,
sexual harassment,

slowdowns,
strikes,

theft,
uniforms and,

white responses to,
and wigging.

Unemployment,
austerity and,

churning and,
confidence and,

depression and,
sense of well-being and,

stagflation.
See also underemployment.

See also relief workers.
Rubber workers,

steel workers,
—black,

numbers in mines and mills,
relations with white workers.

Workers School,
working class,

see also *Worker Writers*.
Lay-offs,

low wages,
conservative climate,

contingent labor,
damaging to,

as artists' subject,
bonded,

children in,
convicts as,

safety and,
affective,

women in,

The woman who disobeyed was built into the city wall but before they completely bricked her in she asked that one arm one eye and one breast remain outside. The wall wept milk and everyone took her in.

On the verge of two collective bargaining agreements I loosen one soaked page from the next. It is August. Month of ascending and descending heat and bank balances.

I return to the archive to ask for more milk for more linear feet and the librarian instructs: "Insert the placeholder in the box so as not to confuse one item with the next." Her badge dangles. I open a file and read a female voice: "We took no cut in pay, we took no cut in holidays. It's not some dream. It did happen. It's not some dream." And another: 1 box 1 linear foot: "To provide short-term positions for unemployed artists."

That spring I slipped on rotting blossoms on the way to work. Sticky petals fell in a courtyard named "shady mistreatment." Under my breath I repeated "you're fine you're hired you're fine you're hired" and I did not fall. Later I asked "what of art and instrumentality?" and as I drew the students out I became drenched by their personalities until love pulled me back.

Question: How to define poverty? Did I mean poetry?

This is about a good job.

Cinder block floor tile ceiling tile. A poster announces "Workers of the World Unite!" and the labor archive is housed in the library's upper floor. The worker behind the desk has a deep cough. The windows do not open and a sign reads "Marxist Study Center." Units of construction. Units of decay: grievances marked with an "X." Plexiglass barriers to prevent the jumpers.

Daily tasks: open a notebook a sketchbook remove the lens cap print out the contract and check for infractions. Arrange the meeting and arrive with a pen saying "I would prefer not to." Draw up plans for a catapult. Teach from a book called *Invisible America*. Discuss the disadvantages of radar the archaeologist's new tool as you take a rusting trowel out of your bag.

If there is an ideology, then the worker is a construction—
If the worker is a construction, then who am I?

If my health benefits cost $316 each month, then is it a benefit?
If these details repel you, then am I a worker and who are you?

If these details repel you, then am I an artist and who are you?
If the archive has a hero, then am I nostalgic?

If there is a cause, then am I troubled?
If Othello cries out "it is the cause, it is the cause"

then is he blind or is he black or both and who are you?
If you call me Norma Rae, then is this a factory and why did I lose?

If the archive is evidence, then why do I play with veils,
repeating "pencil, subterfuge, trail"?

The archaeologist with tenure places a medical waste box at the edge of the brackish water.

The self-appointed inspector drops each grievance tied up with string and marked with an "X" into the box until the box is full.

The teacher who is also an artist slips a complaint under the inspector's door.

The inspector uses her old keys to enter the building and an office at night that is the archaeologist's office by day.

The teaching artist writes in her sketchbook. She conducts research in the archive and discovers her own grievance. She takes the paper that bears her name and eats it. Her vision will blur. She builds a catapult and draws women in flight.

The archaeologist leaves a copy of her autobiography on the corner of the desk knowing that at night the inspector cannot resist reading the manuscript entitled *My Seneca Village*.

Identifying marks: There are none because the cinderblock walls do not give way under the artist's fingers. Because the archaeologist positions the ground penetrating radar above the remains of the school above the remains of the town over which the park was built. Because no soil is disturbed. Because the library's marble floor is too hard for the inspector's body.

Because before each
interview I sew my bank statement under the skin of my hand and shake.

The inspector named Sadie turns the key and enters then presses the soft numbers of the alarm. Once she worked during the day until they wrote "due to" "not able to renew your" "we regret."

Formerly an historian now self-appointed inspector she says "I will sidle right up to their stink and let it be known" without a trace of youthful sibilance. "I will not turn fifty with grace."

This is not quite a hospital not exactly a museum almost a prison and nearly a school. Sadie after stepping over the threshold inhales. The glass doors close behind her and reflect her own body that she mistakes for another each time. Thin and pale she is a hallway she is a blank form a potential grievance eating up her own outline and always arriving.

1st Verbal Step, 2nd Verbal Step, 1st Written Step, 2nd Written Step, Outcome, Arbitration, Signed and Dated, Standard Grievance, Filed.

What would I say to her? "Here is my list." And what would she say in response? "I have a form for these" or "you naïve young thing." But Sadie is always across the lobby down the hall out the door. Or I look up and see her on the library's upper floor. Or I walk in and she is on her way out.

Finally we cross at the elevator's narrow gap. A button pinned to her blouse reads "Women: Don't Agonize, Organize!" I notice a hole around the metal pin and the button has flopped down from its own weight. I hand her my list quickly. She unfolds the paper and the doors close between us.

A strip of unglued veneer hangs from the edge of her desk. Sadie's sweater catches on this bit of damage often until one night she grabs it and pulls it off. "Cheap shit nothing but cheap shit."

There are three designations to affix to each document: "R" "A" or "N" for "Reciprocal" "Antagonistic" "Neutral" to describe the relationship of workplace and worker and boss. Then each grievance is folded then tied and marked on the outside with an "X" for "finished."

Her tiny room and its papers throb. There is one name on the door but two women inside who will meet only twice and the second time will be the end.

[1.1]
Veiling:

Total up all the linear feet in the archive. Go to
midtown and buy the corresponding yardage in
transparent fabrics—curtain sheers, veils, bridal
whites—and place these billowing textures over
the documents, over the shelves in the labor
archive, tucked into box lids, tucked into the
spaces between the boxes.

Wait until dusk before photographing. To soften
the words "hero" and "activist."

Question: Can I get permission to do this?

[1.2]
Shrapnel:

Photograph the archive's twisted scraps. Open the
box lid carefully. Lift them out. Inspect. Put them
back.

Go home and purchase three of your own from
the internet. Arrange the shrapnel in the shadow
archive growing inside your studio.

Pick one up and press it against your cheek. Place
the warm metal in the palm of the hand of the
person to your left. You are in a classroom. Or
the unemployment office. A soup line. Or if time

is moving backwards, you are in the Abraham
Lincoln brigade, fighting the fascists in Spain, and
when you come home you are called a "Red" and
blacklisted.

[1.3]
Lesson:

A war will always enter the archive to structure
the enemy.

[1.4]
Place the following evidence in a folder labeled
"Evidence":

A study conducted in 2009 found that persistent
perceived job insecurity was a powerful predictor
of poor health and might even be more damaging
than actual job loss.

[1.5]
Write an email entitled "Enough is Enough":

After "Dear" continue with "I find it impossible
to continue" or "though you have overpaid me I
am unable to write checks back to you."

Shaking, writing through the membrane that
keeps you both contained, the computer screen
is your new muscle, your wide-open eyes. But

there is little comfort in the sound of "enough is enough." Like a diver about to jump, you see the bottom clearly. You press "send."

The archeologist with tenure named J. collects as many of the old card catalogue cabinets as she can hauling them back to her basement office one by one. Her manuscript also grows an unbound stack on the corner of the desk she shares with Sadie.

My Seneca Village Chapter 1

My story begins when the Parks Department
removed the sign.

Begins with radar. Begins with no soil
disturbed.

My story begins with their new logo
affixed to signs that I commence to
remove with my trowel, un-branding.

What was Seneca Village and who are you?

My Seneca Village Chapter 2

Purchased farmland. Purchased three lots.
Purchased six lots. Purchased twelve
lots. Three churches. Several Cemeteries.
Homes. A School.

Begin by introducing students to the
use of hand-written documents as a way
of discovering the past. Underneath the
logo. Underneath "Wasteland." "Shanties."
"Bloodsuckers." "Insects."

If you know where to look it is possible
to touch Manhattan's first significant
community of African-American property
owners.

```
Rationale: to explore the personal side
of history.

I told the students to bend down like
kneeling and touch the cornerstone of
the only visible remains: a school.
```

Miranda the teaching artist blurs her vision nearly closing her eyes in the corridors upon entering the institution. She runs her fingers over the cinderblocks that lead to the wall panel that frames the metal elevator button. As she waits for the sound of doors opening she presses against the feeling that her clothes may be out of place her posture failing.

*Notes for drawings entitled*
*"Not Everyone Will be Taken into*
*the Future":*

*1. Those who are the takers.*
*2. Those who are taken.*
*3. Those who will not be taken.*

*Titles:*

*1. Incident at the Revolving Door*
*2. Hello, Morning of My Full Employment!*
*3. Altar of W-2s Destroyed by B-52s*
*Destroyed by ...*

Miranda senses another body to her right. The smell of perfume then the click of the elevator button pressed in quick succession three times three times again.

J. presses the button three times. Her finger bends back from the force of her pressure. She presses again in three pulses this time using her thumb to brace her hand. "This place is fucked up fucked up." Waiting she puts her hand in her right pocket and stirs her keys remembering her father. How many times he did things he did not want to do. "Sometimes you just got to you just got to."

Sadie takes the stairs. "Won't catch me getting in there." She pulls at a hangnail nearly bleeding on the edge of her thumb.

I walked into the hallway through the glass doors on the first warm day of the year. I reached out my hand to place the tip of my finger on the cool metal but I did not press. A veil between the elevator and my body came down in a rush of white light. I smelled another woman's conspicuous perfume. I walked away and never returned.

I stayed. But entered the classrooms surrounded by this light an altered vision making my movements slow inserting time between receiving their emails and hitting "reply." I did not agree with everything. I also did not disagree. They could no longer tell.

Into her open mouth Miranda stuffs the paper she no longer reads. Needs. The grievance the gag order the settlement her file her notes on the destruction of the institution.

Miranda's name begins with "to see." Her name falls out of a mouth starting with the sound for "mother" and ending with "ah."

I reach over the table to pull the papers out of her mouth. "Come on open up give them to me." She agrees opens and I reach in. I take her documents peel the wet pages apart and place them to dry in the sun.

*Notes for Catapult:*

*Strung up with four rubbery bands,*
*4 metal coils, a leather harness,*
*broken sheetrock, blue sky above,*
*political posters on the wall,*
*sheetrock crumbles on the floor,*
*shoes left behind, slats in the wall*
*to look in on the scene.*

*Questions:*

*Has the artist left from her studio?*
*Is this a classroom catapult? The library?*
*The faculty lounge? A childhood house?*

Miranda is still hungry. I don't know how to solve this. I look at my eyes in the mirror as I wash her spit from my hands. "I quit you."

Sadie would shout the slogan "There's So Few of Him and So Many of Us!" J. would say "Thank god I'm not you."

Miranda would swallow. I want to make her speak.

No. 004403 / Tamiment Library & Robert F. Wagner Labor Archives / Reader's Card / Name: _____.

I entered the archive and looked for my name. Instead I found the red of certain fonts an international idea the worker. Feeling unorganized unscholarly I gave the librarian my card and in order to keep my loneliness a secret I smiled for her.

Instructions: pick up a pass at the information desk and carry it with you wherever you go. Tell the guards you are heading toward thousands of linear feet of radical America. Child of a Soviet refugee I do not drop my anchor instead I open my notebook writing "Schematic or shelter. Neither."

November 4, 2007: I went to vote and then went to look for the meaning of radical and found myself at home scrolling through the archive's electronic finding guide. In front of the screen my body no longer registered basic needs: food movement water. Weeks later I pushed away stood up and presented the proper identification. I was in.

The librarian brings me the first box: Asian Garment Workers In New York City Oral History Collection, 1 box .5 linear feet.

Second box: Helena Born Papers, 1 box .25 linear feet. Found pressed between the pages of her memoir: a small fern.

Third: Nelson Rollin Burr Papers, 3 boxes 2 linear feet. A collection of 1,300 index cards containing quotations gleaned from selected newspapers relating to labor issues.

Fourth: Israel and Sadie Amter Papers, 1 box .25 linear feet.

I fill out a photocopy request form and wait to take away her poems.

"I dedicate you to the revolution my son."
"Isn't the Soviet Union great?"

First archival disappointment.

"I want no space between lines."

[2.1]
Create a ritual space for the end of *LABOR*:

Take bank statements from the past five years and enlarge. Transform into blueprints and tile a whole wall with the paper that will turn brown. These posters announce a big life change. "The writing is on the wall," as they say.

[2.2]
Create tapestries:

Embroider lists of all the jobs you have ever had. Use your handwriting. Write "worked for a furrier, picked strawberries, taught gymnastics, tried to place refugees in jobs during the last recession." Hang these soft lists from the ceiling.

[2.3]
Place your own documents in the labor archive:

Query the head librarian as to whether they will accept your box of documents. Contents: a copy of the gag order and final settlement, numerous letters of part-time appointments, photographs of the ceremony marking the end of your art, a handful of political buttons from the first Clinton campaign, several notebooks, and various works on paper. 1 box .75 linear feet.

If the archive says "Yes," carry your box to the library and ask if they will allow you to film the transaction. You will hand over your box and watch the librarian take it away.

If the archive says "No," take the letter of refusal and put it in the box with the other documents. Take this box down to the edge of the brackish water and dump out its contents. Film this.

When you're done filming, climb onto the rocks and gather up as many pieces of paper as you can. Put them in the trash can by the fence at the water's edge.

[2.4]
Alternate action:

Take the box of documents to the park and walk into the woods. Find a good spot, preferably under a tree. Take out your trowel and dig a hole. Put the contents of your box in the hole and cover over with earth.

[2.5]
Alternate action 2:

Go to the archive, order up the two files that would be next to your file, alphabetically, and

insert your documents between these files. This
act of corruption is not recommended if you fear
your research privileges will be revoked.

[2.6]
If, on the way to the archive, you meet your
former boss who announces:

"I am the labor archive scholar in residence" and
then asks "What are you doing here?" present
him with your box, open the lid, and invite him
to reach inside and touch this brand new primary
source.

Jobless inspector the architect of her true calling Sadie descends into the subway in morning light. The archaeologist comes up the stairs and walks past Sadie who notes this woman's heavy bag an appendage monogrammed with "J." They nearly touch.

Later that day J. slips her trowel underneath a sign in the hallway and lifts. It comes off easily. She repeats this action down the hall. She repeats this action week after week. Her basement office houses this growing collection the pieces of the institution she has removed.

```
My Seneca Village Chapter 3

Go over the information in "The Present
Look of Our Great Central Park," from
The New-York Daily Times, July 9, 1856.

(By reading between the lines.)

In "City Items: Central Park Lands," from
The New-York Daily Tribune, May 28, 1856.

(Because they need to know how broken.
Because they do not care.)

Go over "Laying of a Corner-Stone"
from The New-York Daily Tribune,
August 5, 1853.

(Because I couldn't find the emotion to
confront the purely wrong.)

Go over "The Present Look of Our Great
Central Park" from The New-York Daily
Times, July 9, 1856.

(By not disturbing the soil.)
```

From her open office door J. watches Miranda search the hall for the right room. "Can I help you?" Miranda does not hear and continues down the hallway eventually finding the classroom. Miranda's fingers skim the cinderblocks. It is the first day and some signs are missing.

Finally inside a classroom Miranda runs her hands over her skirt to smooth any wrinkles and writes "Public Art" on the whiteboard. She sits down to wait for the students and opens her sketchbook.

*Self-portraits in Brutalist architecture:*

*1. Stop and lick the building's wounds.*
*2. Pull the loose insulation from the seams.*
*3. Lift the door back onto its hinges.*
*4. Drain the courtyard puddle.*
*5. Pull at loose wires.*

*Self-portraits in the soft archive:*

*1. Some fabrics say wealthy.*
*2. How to smooth hair.*
*3. Sweaters to avoid.*
*4. Sweaters to afford.*
*5. Wrinkles to prevent.*
*6. Cut clothes into strips.*
*7. Use as warp and weft.*

Miranda asks the students to place their feet on the floor to close their eyes then open their sketchbooks then write. J. stops outside the door and looks in and will continue following Miranda's syllabus all semester as her autobiography falls apart.

I break with the walls I break with the signs and the bindings. I never find the right room and I do not roll off all of the lint. My syllabus stays undone stays secret. My lips cracked the heel of my boot worn through my notebook is finished so I must use scraps of paper I forage. Their assignments their attendance unmarked. My mother's worst fear: "Never let them see you sweat." I stain. I let my eyebrows grow wild and wait for the planners to recoil.

"Are not able to offer" "next semester" "unfortunately due to"

April 20, 2008: "What to give up: art."

March 14, 2009: "The last art for a long time."

April 5-7, 2013: "Countering Contingency: Teaching, Scholarship, and Creativity in the Age of the Adjunct. Call for Proposals."

Miranda told the class she was tired. Miranda unsaid: "I don't remember the last thing I saw clearly."

I saw her bag spill and helped her gather up the books their spines broken. Pens. An empty plastic bottle and one red folder. Keys. The students stepped around her sketchbook.

Miranda would not hope or stand. She spread her arms and legs out across the tiles nearly spanning the width of the corridor repeating "not permissible this is not permitted." Disgusted I walked away.

I stayed. Laid my body down. The tips of our fingers touched as I closed my eyes as a door opened as I heard footsteps and felt his eyeglasses fall as he bent over to look.

His office opens to his assistant's office. The assistant's office opens to three other assistants. The room with the many assistants has a door and on this door is the sign "Dean." They have windows and their own hallway. Not all doors have signs.

Today he swings a door open the door without a sign that leads to the public hallway directly into his expansive office with a wooden desk with a glass table and bookshelves with chairs of leather and enough seats for five people under a large abstract painting that is mostly red.

> *Notes for "The Big Archive."*
>
> *Wood, steel, sheetrock,*
> *3 rooms, 3 corridors,*
> *string, desks, metal chairs,*
> *boxes, official forms, faxes.*
>
> *"The Big Archive, Version 2."*
>
> *All documents hang from the ceiling*
> *just out of reach.*
>
> *"The Toilet."*
>
> *Stone, cement, wood,*
> *"Women" sign, porcelain fixtures,*
> *household objects, hangers,*
> *glass bottles, white lace.*
>
> *"A Room Taking off in Flight."*

*Wood, steel, fabric construction,*
*spiral staircase, partitioned rooms,*
*school furniture, books, gaping hole,*
*a second gaping hole, a third.*

He bursts out into the hallway. Miranda says "excuse me" and he tilts his head as if trying to remember her then scurries off without saying anything his torso pitched forward.

I crossed the thresholds that lead to his office. We shook hands. I sat under the famous painting. He opened his computer and I watched his eyes flick back and forth watched him swivel around to pick up my resume from his printer saying "here you are." He took time to glance at my document and I looked down at my wrist bone my fingers and rings. I uncapped my pen. I saw a book with a gold award sticker on his desk and I tried to read as many other names as I could. I had covered up my tattoo. He looked out from above his glasses. I wore my best pants. I brought my voice down to a lower register as he leaned back in his chair and asked "Do you have children?" "Where do you live?" and again "Do you have children?"

And then he asked Miranda again "do you have children?" and again when they rode the elevator together to which she finally roared "I do not have sex that way." Or she stayed contained believing he might grant her a good position yet.

The boss confesses how badly he would like to lick the envelope that holds a copy of the latest grievance. Sadie explains "there's nothing to lick." "Put your finger here."

Four floors above her he felt lonely and knew that if he came looking she would let him in. He wanted to come down to express his good politics his sorry.

Inside her nighttime office sitting in an extra chair whose back is broken he puts his finger down on top of a grievance that rests on top of a manuscript entitled *My Seneca Village*. Sadie loops the string quickly catching the tip of his finger until he pulls away and the knot is tight. About the manuscript he asks "Is this yours?"

"Ours."

```
My Seneca Village Chapter 4

For the opening and laying out of a
public place.

(How can you bloom so fresh. How? Your
womb is coming out of your head. Put it
back.)

An act to alter the map. To authorize
the taking.

(How can you so discredited so bloom?
Do you still want to know how to heal
others?

Thank you, but I can no longer speak.)
```

```
Is bounded southerly, northerly,
easterly, and west.

(Is this an improvement is this my stupid
archeology? He is afraid to talk to me to
touch me to return me to the university.)

(Our office your complaint my security.
My security can not look at her or her
even though I see.)

(I, no longer school.

Their glances across the room, from
across the conference table, in the
elevator. Who invited them?

Their stupid too-much blood, my
tightening silence, their messy sacrifice,
my pay stub.

I, the right one, they say, no longer
know how to write.)
```

Sadie is white. More than Miranda and not like J.

Theory may be below ground or worn on the skin for example students request extra time for their assignments to which J. says "no absolutely not" resulting in a complaint and a meeting. But she is not interested in nurturing or finding a home place at work.

J. speaks confidently with credentials. She wears her I.D. around her neck always and a suit so as not to be stopped at the threshold of the mailbox room. "Are you faculty?"

An undergraduate slouches and stretches his legs out from the first row toward her so that if she wanted to circulate around the room she would have to step over him or beg his pardon.

The carpet is ripped in spots and there is a layer of condensation working its way down from the top of the windows that look out into a courtyard made of concrete slabs. This courtyard does not drain properly.

J. begins with the story of Seneca Village. The student flips his pencil around the fingers of his right hand. She turns away she touches her laptop to get to the next slide. When she turns again to face the class his mouth is slightly open and he is looking at her body. J. turns back to face her computer. She teaches from the textbook called *Invisible America*.

When she turns to face the class again she says "we'll break early today that's fine." J. turns her computer off unscrews the cable packs up her briefcase and leaves the projector on ignoring the sign "PLEASE TURN ALL EQUIPMENT OFF."

[3.1]
Move your finger down the list:

Decipher the 19th century handwritten record of property ownership. Count how many African-Americans owned plots of land in Manhattan, between 82nd and 89th Streets and Seventh and Eighth Avenues. Your finger traces the history of Central Park, urban planning, wealth, and eminent domain.

You are not in the labor archive. You are reading "Seneca Village: A Teacher's Guide to Using Primary Sources in the Classroom."

[3.2]
A census:

264 people lived in Seneca Village in 1855. After the birth of the idea of Central Park, newspapers called it "Nigger Village."

[3.3]
Take the blurry photo into your hands:

A black child is playing with a white child. Coffins were later dug up.

[3.4]
In the present tense:

Brush the earth from the stone.

A professor returns to the site with her class and sees that the sign is now gone. There is a long silence. She stands with her hands in her pockets. "If you look at the ground closely, here, where the earth dips down from a landscaped knoll, you can see a cornerstone. This was the school. Go ahead, bend down and touch it."

When it is your turn, you brush away some earth from the stone and watch a tiny ant scurry across.

There are different versions of Sadie's transgression. In one she stops showing up to teach. The class is called "Radical America." In another version she slams his door so hard that the famous painting falls off the wall its frame cracks.

Now she walks down to the edge of the brackish water to place a bundle of documents into a metal box with a small slot on top. "Hazardous Medical Waste." But after one year of this ritual near the empty pit where the World Trade Center used to be and working conditions that are in no way improving Sadie stops making her trips to the water. Her clothes sag. "Let that fucking box rot."

Pressed into more action Sadie takes the documents and inserts them into the boxes of the labor archive. She locates the right place according to alphabetical order and calls up the file on either side and places the new one between. Her alien files devoid of call numbers a corruption a surprise.

At the sound of another red folder sliding under the door Sadie quickly opens to find J. facing her saying "thank you for your work."

"Do you know about the drop box?"

"Yes I put it there. Did you read my autobiography?"

"I do."

I inventory the range of narrative problems:

What does J. get from Sadie and what does Miranda get from J.?
How does J. know to place the dropbox at the water's edge?

Why will Miranda go looking for her grievance in the archive?
Why should I stop Miranda from eating her file?

Where do they learn to slip red folders under Sadie's door?
How does Miranda know that Sadie is J.'s double, their office the same?

How does Sadie find the dropbox and why does J. turn to poetry?
Why won't the boss take away Sadie's keys?

Because an autobiography is a guidebook disintegrating
and Sadie reads nothing between the lines. Miranda will.

Because Miranda will never see J. but knows she is there.
Because she never needed the signs that J. takes away.

Because I cannot unbraid Reciprocal, Antagonistic, and Neutral.

Because trucks took pieces of the ruin to the pier
at the edge of the brackish water and everyone saw.

Because after the attack Sadie watched the boss
receive treatments along with everyone else.

I want J. to step across the threshold to their office and tell Sadie to pack up and leave to insist that her project is over. But before J. can say anything more Sadie takes a step back and shuts the door and J. will never knock again though the boss will come down and Sadie will let him in. I want Miranda to enter to help them all but she refuses to linger inside this architecture.

Back in the archive I fill out more slips. The librarian brings box after box to my table.

Fifth Box: Barbara Kopple Peekskill Riots Photographs UNPROCESSED COLLECTION stored in two boxes. Note: images of Robeson at a distance. Sixth Box: Tuli Kupferberg Radical Humor Collection, 1 box .25 linear feet. Seventh Box: Alex Bittleman *Things I have Learned* typescript. 4 boxes 2 linear feet. Eighth Box: George Breitman Oral History Collection Public Programs. SCOPE AND CONTENT NOTE: Series I: Malcolm X and other personalities. Index available in repository. Ninth Box: Camp Midvale/ Nature Friends of America. 1 box .5 linear feet. The collection contains documents of FBI investigations into the actions of the camp obtained through a Freedom of Information Act request.

I want more but worry that the librarian has figured out that I have no research plan so I leave with no photocopies no discoveries.

A man a scholar sitting at a table with stacks of books and a rolling cart next to him containing four archive boxes and laptop open watches me pack up my notebook my pencil. I put on my jacket and tie my scarf. Walking toward the glass doors I feel too tall. I look over at the librarian who must buzz me out and I wait until she notices. The click of the door behind me the hush of the atrium. Windows on all sides. Marble floor eight stories below.

The records show that there was no inspection performed to note the gap in the plexiglass barrier system. Small fissure around the stairwells and enough distance from the edge to fit a body between and then let go. "There was no blood."

The planners gathered at the site at 7:30 in the morning saying the words "the university wellness hotline" and "free counseling" as often as possible.

```
              My Seneca Village Chapter ___

              After eloquent speeches

                                  Was dug up

              While laborers              uprooting

              Decayed almost to a skeleton         she

                       Fourteen inches beneath

                           A new entrance

              Enclosing the body of a negro
              on the lid a plate richly mounted

                       aged sixteen years

                           At a short distance
                   another coffin found

              Lies a neat little settlement


              (If they had allowed an excavation, my
              Seneca Village would be)
```

Cameras swarmed the entrance to the library. Sadie paused with the others and listened to the planners say "he was a sophomore" and "at approximately 4:30 in the morning" and she remembered where she had been then in the basement at work bundling more grievances to be filed. It was a Tuesday. A reporter asked "had the barriers been inspected recently?"

At home Sadie drew the blinds she took off her clothes and slipped inside the envelope of blanket and sheet but she did not sleep. How to ease the vertigo. How to be held to be open without breaking the binding in the cradle not sadistic to be held and not to fall—

I lift Sadie out of the box carefully reading "You will win this great battle!" but I am too shy to write in all caps as she has done. I pull a gauzy veil up over her documents revising Sadie whispering

Only use pencil
to rest your documents
to sleep
to splay
safely this cradle—

[4.1]
Photograph:

Walk into the elevator with camera in hand, held
low. Press 8 for the archive, inconspicuously.
Insert the document of this vertigo back into the
archive's boxes.

[4.2]
Blur:

Hold the video camera at waist height by placing
it inside a cloth book bag with a hole cut out,
just big enough for the lens. Walk through halls
in the darkening sub-basement level. Past the
archaeologist's office. Past the occasional security
keypads placed at eye level.

[4.3]
Copy:

By hand, each page of the archive's finding guide.
Optional: videotape this performance.

[4.4]
Record:

Your voice reading from the archive's finding
guide. Read each name, the call numbers, the
number of boxes, linear feet, and the description.

Optional: if you film this, allow your face, reading, to come in and out of focus.

[4.5]
Camera:

Assemble the tripod at the end of the hall. Look through the lens and find the crosshairs. The horizontal line is intersected by your body and your ancestors.

[4.6]
Create your own offer of tenure:

An offer of tenure may be written, typed up, and printed out on institutional letterhead, folded, addressed to you, stamped, mailed, ripped open, and accepted.

Unfold this letter and soak in tea for an historical look. You are ahead of your time.

Place this letter in a file folder labeled "My Employment."

Miranda finds Sadie at the edge of the plexiglass barrier standing at the fissure. She says "go ahead."

Miranda files a grievance. She wins.

Miranda files a grievance. Nothing happens.

Miranda tosses her sketchbooks into the brackish water. She slips a complaint under Sadie's door. Nothing happens.

Miranda gives every student an "A" and pays none of her bills.

Miranda finds Sadie at the edge about to leap into the atrium and says "you must not." She takes hold of Sadie's arm tightly.

>           *Notes for "Line of Flight":*
>
>           *After accusations, in total despair,*
>           *having opened the balcony door,*
>           *the woman steps out near dawn*
>           *to get some fresh air.*
>
>           *Suddenly, she sees that in the sky,*
>           *which is beginning to lighten,*
>           *there are people hovering in the air.*
>
>           *Either they descend down near the ground*
>           *or they rise up high, so high*
>           *they almost become invisible;*

*they either fly alone*
*or in pairs or in groups, or,*
*clasping hands, they form rings,*
*which slowly revolve.*

*Hovering between them*
*are things of their everyday existence.*

*The woman sees another woman she knows,*
*flying, and waves her arms then pushes off*
*and takes off flying after her.*

*They clasp hands.*

[5.1]
A workshop:

In the place of a poetry reading or gallery exhibit, discuss strategies for surviving in the city. It is a workshop on finances. Each person tells how they do it. Possible title: "Art is Expensive." Exchange a scarf. Bring some baked goods to sell or share.

[5.2]
A scantron:

is used to evaluate the teacher's work at the end of the semester. Run the results through voice recognition software and play into the space of your studio. The monotone computerized voice will suggest a chant.

[5.3]
X axis, Y axis:

Create a grid. One axis is "sentimental." The other is "real." Chart a worker/hero from the archive. This is a portrait. The reader may locate herself.

At the edge of the campus is a forest. Miranda enters and blurs her eyes. She waits for the feel of the path before moving forward. New leaves brush against her face as she makes her way to a circle of grass matted down by deer. She takes off her clothes and spreads her body out down at the limit of the earth. Memory of the forest at the edge of her great-grandmother's village where she walked in and found her first clearing and did the same.

*Notes for "The Clearing":*

*Poorly lit corridor.*
*Shafts of sunlight reach the forest floor.*
*Which curriculum is yours?*

*Take off your clothes.*
*Put on your daughter.*

*The buzz of hanging light bulbs.*
*The sound of the grass.*

*A narrow wooden walkway begins*
*at the edge of the forest and continues*
*toward the clearing. Visitors walk on it*
*and eventually reach the clearing*
*where the walkway elevates into a bridge*
*and they may look down and view you*
*or your re-enactor*
*but not for long because others want to see*
*and because the bridge is narrow,*
*they are forced to keep moving.*

*The narrow wooden bridge*
*makes a sharp turn toward the left*
*away from your body*
*or this woman's body*
*and leads the onlookers out of the forest.*
*At the end of the walkway*
*at the entrance to the village*
*there is a sign:*

*"And where would you drop your anchor?"*


Back inside called to a meeting she notes the excess of red paint at the bottom of the canvas. Between them her crossed legs her desire for money. He mistakes this for a desire for him. After promising her nothing he comes close to touching her hand for emphasis for empathy. She watches his hand shift from his thigh toward hers.

That night Miranda sits in a small room where some pay a price to talk with her privately and show her pages of their sketchbook to confess their fears about being an artist. This takes place in an old warehouse in a part of the city that used to be cheap. Beyond the edge of affordability it is called "The Art Brothel."

Ten dollars for fifteen minutes or twenty for thirty or forty for an hour. They enter in sessions and breathe on her neck as they move in closer to show her their sketchbooks. They smell of cigarettes and beer and sex.

Down the stairs eventually outside she walks away and wraps her fingers around a pocket full of cash. Memory of his unwashed body and how she let him go on talking about painting and wringing his skinny hands his fingernails dirty then folding his arms saying "you know it's like I have always been an artist you know?"

"No I don't."

My Seneca Village Chapter ____

Manhattan Square Benefit Map. Central Park Condemnation Map.

Blocks 780 to 782. Class Discussion.

The Families of William Godfrey Wilson and Andrew Williams. An Affidavit of Petition. Christopher Rush. Leven Smith. Thomas McClure.

Class Discussion. For part of a public street. Blocks 783 to 785. Blocks 789 to 790.

Burial (colored). Marriage (colored, white). For Class Discussion. For a part of the public street.

My Seneca Village Chapter ____
Version 2

Who is allowed. Only comfort. Who is allowed to be on fire. To be named. Who

is allowed to be black. Who is allowed
to be without. Who is allowed to be read
who is allowed to be soft petals.

And what if I am not?

The high pitch of pretty the sureness
of occupy. Who is allowed to be business
and just the facts the rot of them—

If it is visual. Only comfort.

It is
as long as I dig.

[6.1]
Film:

The filmmaker stands outside the frosted-over
factory windows, some of which are open a crack
and the workers look out. It is the day of the plant
closing. A woman appears through one open
window, she is a public relations executive, and
she does not let him in. She instructs the security
guard: "Please remove him."

Revise this scene so that he smashes the windows,
enters, and declares his alliance.

In this new version of the film, the filmmaker
does not make fun of the woman who is trying
to make money consulting other women on their
color palette in her Michigan living room.

[6.2]
Film 2:

Elsewhere, on a dirt road, another filmmaker
presents a warrant for the gun thug's arrest. There
is a scuffle. She is audible off camera. "We shall
overcome." Next to the workers' wives, singing,
I hear her New York accent.

Make a new version where, after the scuffle, she instructs everyone to get in the car, turns off the cameras, they leave for New York, for safety, and the film is never made.

From the courtyard it is possible to see up into his large office. This is a building without skin. Miranda sits below.

*Possible drawings. Tuesday 10:21 am:*

*1. The Man Who Collected the Opinions of Others.*
*2. The Man Who Flew into Space from His Apartment.*
*3. The Short Man.*
*4. The Man of Many Suits.*
*5. The Man Who Never Threw Anything Away.*
*6. The Man Who Collected the Names of Mothers.*

*Alternates:*

*The woman who, being tasted.*
*The woman who, only her legs.*

*Her gray-lined skull.*
*Her lucky little owl.*

*Beautiful retina, her archeology.*

I look up. He looks down and starts pacing the length of his office. His cell phone in his hand and pressed against his face. I write "to hate one's big job is possible."

Later in the classroom the old cemetery across the street occupies a sliver of my vision.

Memory of visiting the formerly occupied Soviet zone: I walked through the ruin next to the abandoned radio tower through the opening without a door into cinder block walls without a roof. A piece of paper slightly crumpled nestled between thistle and goldenrod pushing up from a crack in the cement and I thought "a document a secret." I reached down for it and as I brought the paper into focus I threw it down quickly shaking my hand ashamed by my eagerness to pick up a piece of paper marked by shit nothing but paper used to wipe.

From the classroom window we watch a young woman scale the wrought-iron cemetery fence. She is at the top a foot on either side the sharp spikes in the middle. Someone says "she's stuck." The young woman climbing notices that we are watching. A student shakes a finger at her yelling from behind the glass of our window "get down!" A policeman walks by on the other side of the street. She does not drop in.

My Seneca Village Chapter ___

Laborer. Domestic. Domestic. Gardener.
Laborer. Domestic. Whether Black or
Mulatto. Owners of land. Pedlar.
Milkman. Servant. Grocer. Servant.
Waiter. Porter. Waiter. Laborer.
Driver.

Whether Deaf, Dumb, Blind, Insane or
Idiotic.

Wife. Child. Child. Child. Boarder.
Wife. Brother. Child. Child. Father.
Wife.

Frame. Frame. Frame. Relation to the
head. Of what material built.

17. 11. 5. 5. 1. 15. 3. 30. 30. 11.
Years resident in this city or town.

Native. Naturalized. Aliens. Ireland.
Germany. Germany. New York. Virginia.
Maryland. New York. New York. France.
New York. New York. New York.


My Seneca Village Chapter ___
Version 2

Not remembering hands.

An x-ray not remembering hands.

It is not the map you need the butterfly
wings. It is the snake.

Blood roses. Gather them from the
basement.

Leading up to a fire is the map you
need. Follow the snake.

Citations now grafting. Read the mark
leading up to she.

Leading up to the collapse, I,

[7.1]
To create rust:

Take offers of adjunct employment and paper clip
them together. Soak in water. Remove the paper
clips. The rust will remain. Place inside a file folder
labeled "Rusty Pages." Drop strands of your hair
into the folder to mimic archival authenticity.

[7.2]
Water damage repair:

Use sheets of paper to trace the stains in the carpet
where water has seeped through. Water: the
archive's nemesis. Take these stain patterns and cut
matching sheets of plywood. Place the plywood
over the rain-damaged places in the floor.

[7.3]
Research living elsewhere:

such as: Mexico City, Portugal, Kentucky. There is
no way to turn around. Tell your friends: "I was one
of three finalists" and "the job was cut to half time"
and "we ran out of money." With the final page of
the employee handbook folded up in your pocket,
the size of a passport, take the leap.

To get to the classroom I walk past the slogan "OCCUPY NOW" written in black marker in the stairwell. I walk past the Weather Underground house and feel time compressing past a university president's house through the courtyard and up the stairs and eventually out toward the brackish water.

The student who admits proudly that the graffiti is his says "the janitors are union and our tuition pays their inflated salaries so fuck 'em"

to which Miranda answers by grabbing her rib cage on both sides and ripping spilling out red running toward his notebook. Linear feet spread. The scramble to pick up papers and books to clear the table. Chairs scrape against the floor. Her eyes are closed.

J. stands outside in the corridor and sees.

*Notes for a film. Thursday 11:05 am:*

*When you are lying in the grass,*
*with your head thrown back,*
*there is no one around you,*
*and only the sound of the wind can be heard*
*and you look up into the open sky—there,*
*up above, is the blue sky and the clouds*
*floating by—*
*perhaps this is the very best thing that you*
*have ever done or seen in your life.*

[8.1]
Ceremony:

Order a custom-made stamp that spells your name
and the words "LABOR ARCHIVE" and with
red ink, stamp the cover of each notebook and
sketchbook you have filled over the years. Place
these artifacts on a long table draped in a white
tablecloth. Build a plexiglass box to cover the books
now stamped in red.

[8.2]
Announce the end of your art:

Invite others to come and pay their respects to the
work on display. Visitors may place plastic flowers—
yellows and blues and pinks—on top of the display
and stand and reflect before they move on, before
they move into the intense sunlight outside.

Plan the ceremony for high noon.

Hire a document disposal company to come and
pick up the notebooks and sketchbooks for eventual
shredding.

[8.3]
Read, out loud:

each page of each contract. You are part-time in
three places, so there are three contracts, totaling
298 pages, including appendices. Perform this in
the courtyard of flowering trees.

[8.4]
Locate yourself:

in the trend toward hiring part-time workers.
Memory: of a father's class action lawsuit against
a company who fired them as they approached
retirement. That was the 80s. The company made
pharmaceuticals and good profits. This is higher
education.

[8.5]
Place a small X:

along the curving line named "part-time
appointments" as it rises. You are the "X."
Overlay this with the curve that rises, called "top
administrative salaries" and "technology costs"
and "health care costs."

[8.6]
Download and print out:

the electronic version of the International
Monetary Fund report that states that after
the 173 recorded instances of fiscal austerity
advanced by countries from 1978 to 2009,
economic contraction and unemployment
ensued. Possible title: *Discolor My Parachute*.

[8.7]
Employ your sociological imagination:

Separate the knowledge of these trends from the
word "complaint," as if you are pulling apart the
strands that make a thread. This thread, the one
you are pulling apart, is a deep red color.

[8.8]
Art and instrumentality:

The planners do not expect that you are able
to split this thread so carefully, and they do
not believe you will use it, taking your needle
and writing your story across the pages of the
employee handbook. You will exhibit this version
of the handbook, your split stitch spilling over
each page.

The old eight-drawer card catalogue cabinet is tagged with "DISCARD."
"Can I have that?" "Are you faculty?" J. removes the I.D. from around her
neck and passes it across the counter for inspection. "Sorry. Sure."

She lifts the cabinet onto her hip and walks across the marble floor
toward the security desk. She imagines a slip. It is evening and dusk and
the city is littered with the petals of spent flowers. Its metal edges press
into her hands. The guard holds out his hand to receive her I.D. and she
presents this to him along with the handwritten note from the librarian
"OK TO TAKE AWAY."

As she presses against the turnstile to exit comes the dull thud of the body
falling fallen behind her then quick screams then the crash of her cabinet
that spills out of her hands as she turns to the sounds. Everything bent
from the trauma. The body is Sadie. Sadie whose reports of wrongdoings
no longer pulse.

```
My Seneca Village Chapter ____

Was a resident, there buried, baptized

Will not stop saying this

When asked if his house could be moved

Will not stop speaking

No record of official response

To walk away, revolution
```

A fall to the center of the earth

Newspapers blow by, reminding me

Of a spine

Of a ball of string

Of a cornerstone, another cornerstone who

Will not stop speaking




I do not know how to help you

Teacher

put your heart back in. Hinge. Must staple you up. Dear Campus

I broke into you. I pull burrs from my hair from your forest. Today I am
that teacher. Dear Curriculum

You limping idea. You limping artist. You perpetual girl. I bracket you
off. Drawing

I love you with your box frame with your blur. Victim I love you because
of the economy because the first letter of my name fell from my keyboard

because my family could not orchestrate an emergence or send down
strong enough shoots. Because I must use the tip of my finger to see—

Because cohort means—

Go perform. And what if I did not?

This is one version of
how I arrived: I walked up the avenue into the air of the Cross Bronx
Expressway into redlining into the history of fires set by absentee
landlords to collect insurance money. This was my first job. I walked away
from a movie called "Fort Apache, the Bronx." Decades later to read to
write and I never felt danger.

I stepped off the train as a teacher walking past the cops up the hill.
Already there was memorial graffiti everyone could read except for me.
Already my failure my hope a youthful "yes." My skin. A lost union vote.

What had I taught? What I had learned. This must be a fiction.

As a deer Miranda is fluid her transformation complete.

My change swiftly into a leap.
Tired of the planners the predators intersecting with prey. Tired by the justice of plot the vote the legible—

I run my hands over fur.

A deer sleeps at the foot of my bed. A sister is down the hall.

As the house grows mold as overgrown grass turns to fur as the archive releases its holdings the flutter of paper in flight I find an empty room and count the nails in the floorboards. I touch the seams in the wallpaper. Planning arranging saying "this is a good place for a work table and shelves." The glass in the window is rippled.

My shadow archive my finding guide grows:

Women on the Job Records. Including Advocacy Kit and Fair Pay Bill material. "They Were Not Silent" (Film) Project Files. Gender Relations in the Building Trades Oral History Collection. RESTRICTED ACCESS. *Communism on Campus: Recollections and Comments of a Former Communist Teacher at CCNY.* Harvard Graduate Student and Teaching Fellows Union Records. Coauthor of *Detroit: I Do Mind Dying.* Chairman of a 1930s Artists' Cooperative. Musical Mutual Protective Union Minutes. Out in the Union: Gays and Lesbians in the Labor Movement. NOTE TO RESEARCHERS: This collection is restricted. Drafts of the poems "To Hell with Hoovers" and "Liberty." New York University Clerical Workers Files. Concerning an unsuccessful organizing campaign. Scenes showing the unemployed and breadlines during the Depression (quality is extremely poor). Cleveland Radicalism Clippings Scrapbook. Of unknown provenance in fragile and fading condition and was disbound and recopied—

Saying "no repair is too much no repair too much" so that when they approach down the hallway through the gate from under the sign from under the logo with an eviction notice with an evaluation form with a sentence a settlement a complaint.

With the snap of branches comes a flash of white light—

What is the opposite of labor of struggle?

Glimmering forested corridors.

J. smashes the window that leads to the courtyard as Miranda leaps through and Sadie wakes up. The archive is on fire and we are faceless. Inside the room without a door the room they never knew we were building a room without maps with pearls lined up in curving rows we finally sit down shake loose our names.

[Epilogue]

Notice the woman on the subway painfully bending sitting slowly holding a clear plastic bag of small bottles of lotion powder shampoo and I wonder why she did not take a cab home from the hospital. Comes an image of two twenty-dollar bills and this image floats between us. After a meeting with a college president who says "there is no money for full-time jobs" and after hearing a recording of Monk in the café I walk away saying "there has always been struggle and beauty struggle and beauty." Assignment: walk past The Village Vanguard on your way to teaching a class where a student talks about Detroit until she turns from the screen in order to cry and we agree to silently read what she has projected. Assignment: Place this manuscript in a folder and feed this folder to a box lined with fur. Alternate: Find a meadow with golden and brown grass in swirls from melted snow and watch clouds race above. Track these pages playfully. Because you have a listening name and love will pull you back.

# NOTES

The archive upon which this fiction is based is the Tamiment Library & Robert F. Wagner Labor Archives, a public archive located in New York University's Bobst Library.

Language in the beginning poem sequence is gleaned from the indexes of the following books: The American Social History Project's *Who Built America: Working People & The Nation's Economy, Politics, Culture & Society, Volume II; Workers' Expressions: Beyond Accommodation and Resistance* edited by John Calagione, Doris Francis, and Daniel Nugent; *Labor of Love, Labor of Sorrow: Black Women, Work, and the Family, from Slavery to the Present* by Jacqueline Jones; Robin D. G. Kelley's *Hammer and Hoe: Alabama Communists During the Great Depression* and *Race Rebels: Culture, Politics, and the Black Working Class;* and Paul Krugman's *End This Depression Now!*

Some language in the "My Seneca Village" sequence is from the booklet "Seneca Village: A Teacher's Guide to Using Primary Sources in the Classroom," published by the New York Historical Society. The story of the mysterious removal of the plaque marking a portion of the Seneca Village site in Manhattan's Central Park is not a fiction. Alice Notley's *Alma, or the Dead Women* is also a source of language in these sections.

Many of the italicized notes in the teaching artist's sketchbook are based on the writings and artworks of Ilya Kabakov collected in Phaidon's *Ilya Kabakov*, edited by Boris Groys, David A. Ross, and Iwona Blazwick.

The story of the woman built into the wall, mentioned on page 14, is based on an Albanian folktale as told by Stefan Çapaliku while he was a writer-in-residence with apexart in New York City.

The line "to provide short-term positions for unemployed artists" on page 14 is from the Wagner Archive/Tamiment Library files of the Comprehensive Employment Training Act: Artists Organization, established in 1973, and comprised of artists in New York City "who fought for job security . . . artists projects, and workers rights."

On page 14 the words "you're fine you're hired" refer to the Lorna Simpson piece "You're Fine."

The quote, "We took no cut in pay, we took no cut in holidays, it's not some dream, it did happen, it's not some dream" on page 14 is taken from a transcript of labor activist and garment worker Katie Quan's 1989 testimony from the Asian Garment Workers in New York City Oral History Collection, housed in the Wagner Archive/Tamiment Library.

On page 15 and 41, *Invisible America* refers to the textbook *Invisible America: Unearthing our Hidden History*, edited by Mark Leone and Neil Asher Silberman.

The quote "I would prefer not to" on page 15 is from Herman Melville's story, "Bartleby, the Scrivener: A Story of Wall-street."

The categories "Reciprocal, Antagonistic, Neutral" on page 20 are based on architect Bernard Tschumi's categories delineated in his book *Event-Cities 3*.

The shrapnel first referred to on page 21 is from an archive of the Abraham Lincoln Brigade, a group of approximately 2,800 U.S. citizens who fought fascism in the Spanish Civil War. The records and memorabilia, including pieces of shrapnel, are housed in the Wagner Archive/Tamiment Library.

The veiling image on page 21 comes, in part, from Robin D. G. Kelley's *Race Rebels: Culture, Politics, and the Black Working Class*. In response to the blind spots of traditional labor studies, particularly regarding workers of color, Kelley implores scholars to look "deeper beyond the veil, beyond the public transcript of accommodation and traditional protest . . ."

Another source for the image of the veil is "The Collections of Barbara Bloom," exhibited at the International Center for Photography in 2008. Bloom hung veils in front of some photographs in the portion of the exhibit entitled "Blushing."

On page 22, the idea of war as something that "structures the enemy" is from a paper by Allen Feldman entitled "The Structuring Enemy and Archival War" presented at the 2010 New School University Memory Conference.

The study referred to on page 22 is quoted in a *New York Times* article entitled "At Closing Plant, Ordeal Included Heart Attacks" by Michael Luo, February 24, 2010.

The reference to Brutalist architecture on page 34 is inspired by a conversation between photographer Nancy Davenport and artist Barbara Pollack published in *Atlantica*.

On page 40, "But she is not interested in nurturing or finding a home place at work" is based on information from "Race, Class and Gender: Black Women In Academia," by Adah L. Ward Randolph, PhD, presented at the 1999 conference "Black Women in the Academy II: Service and Leadership."

The film image of a face coming in and out of focus on page 51 is based on artist Linda Montano's 1977 video "Mitchell's Death."

The films referred to on pages 59 and 60 are Michael Moore's 1989 "Roger and Me" and Barbara Kopple's 1976 "Harlan County U.S.A."

On page 61, "a building without skin" refers to the article "Skinless Architecture" by Beatriz Colomina.

The International Monetary Fund report information on page 69 is taken from Paul Krugman's book *End this Depression Now!*

On page 69, the "sociological imagination" is a concept defined by C. Wright Mills in his seminal book *The Sociological Imagination*, published first in 1959. Mills writes: "The first fruit of this imagination—and the first lesson of the social science that embodies it—is the idea that the individual can understand his own experience and gauge his own fate only by locating himself within his period, that he can know his own chances in life only by becoming aware of those of all individuals in his circumstances. In many ways it is a terrible lesson; in many ways a magnificent one."

"Glimmering forested corridors" on page 76 is from Jackson Mac Low's *154 Forties*.

In the Epilogue, the phrase "you have a listening name" is from Alice Notley's *Alma, or the Dead Women*.

## ACKNOWLEDGEMENTS

I am grateful to Rebecca Brown, Douglas A. Martin, and Bhanu Kapil for their guidance and teachings, especially Bhanu who directed me to the Grosz, Colomina, and Tschumi texts. Thanks to John Calagione who first suggested I write an "alternative" employee handbook. I extend gratitude also to Stephen Motika for his passionate editing, and, finally, to Sherine Gilmour for helping me find and tell this story in order not just to survive, but to thrive.

Portions of *LABOR* have been published in somewhat different forms in *The Brooklyn Rail, jubilat, Peep Show, Rattapallax,* and *SET*. A performance document based on the work was published in Ugly Duckling Presse's *EMERGENCY INDEX 2012*. Thanks to those editors for their support.

The embroidery on the cover is from the series "LABOR: What is the Meaning of My No?" installed at the Brooklyn Textile Arts Center in July of 2011. I am grateful to the staff and fellow resident artists there for creating a generative space.

This book is dedicated to every student I have worked with, to my union brothers and sisters, to everyone who struggles in the face of austerity policies and egregious inequality, and to our artists who persist in making sense and beauty, still. Most of all, this book is for Jonny, for walking into the forest with me.

*LABOR* is a fiction. Except for the real of the archive,
the book's people, places, and events are imagined.

## NIGHTBOAT BOOKS

Nightboat Books, a nonprofit organization, seeks to develop audiences for writers whose work resists convention and transcends boundaries. We publish books rich with poignancy, intelligence, and risk. Please visit our website, www.nightboat.org, to learn about our titles and how you can support our future publications.

The following individuals have supported the publication of this book. We thank them for their generosity and commitment to the mission of Nightboat Books:

Kazim Ali
Elizabeth Motika
Benjamin Taylor

In addition, this book has been made possible, in part, by a grant from the New York State Council on the Arts Literature Program.

NYSCA